Poems of the Past and the Present

Thomas Hardy

Poems of the Past and the Present

ISBN: 978-1-63637-954-8

CONTENTS

IMITATIONS, Etc.

RETROSPECT

V. R. 1819–1901

A REVERIE

Moments the mightiest pass uncalendared,
   And when the Absolute
 In backward Time outgave the deedful word
   Whereby all life is stirred:
"Let one be born and throned whose mould shall constitute
The norm of every royal-reckoned attribute,"
   No mortal knew or heard.
 But in due days the purposed Life outshone—
   Serene, sagacious, free;
  —Her waxing seasons bloomed with deeds well done,
   And the world's heart was won . . .
Yet may the deed of hers most bright in eyes to be
Lie hid from ours—as in the All-One's thought lay she—
   Till ripening years have run.

Sunday Night,
27th January 1901

WAR POEMS

EMBARCATION

(Southampton Docks: October, 1899)

Here, where Vespasian's legions struck the sands,
And Cerdic with his Saxons entered in,
And Henry's army leapt afloat to win
Convincing triumphs over neighbour lands,

Vaster battalions press for further strands,
To argue in the self-same bloody mode
Which this late age of thought, and pact, and code,
Still fails to mend.—Now deckward tramp the bands,
Yellow as autumn leaves, alive as spring;
And as each host draws out upon the sea
Beyond which lies the tragical To-be,
None dubious of the cause, none murmuring,

Wives, sisters, parents, wave white hands and smile,
As if they knew not that they weep the while.

DEPARTURE

(Southampton Docks: October, 1899)

While the far farewell music thins and fails,
And the broad bottoms rip the bearing brine—
All smalling slowly to the gray sea line—
And each significant red smoke-shaft pales,

Keen sense of severance everywhere prevails,
Which shapes the late long tramp of mounting men
To seeming words that ask and ask again:
"How long, O striving Teutons, Slavs, and Gaels
Must your wroth reasonings trade on lives like these,
That are as puppets in a playing hand?—
When shall the saner softer polities
Whereof we dream, have play in each proud land,
And patriotism, grown Godlike, scorn to stand
Bondslave to realms, but circle earth and seas?"

THE COLONEL'S SOLILOQUY

(Southampton Docks: October, 1899)

"The quay recedes. Hurrah! Ahead we go! . . .
It's true I've been accustomed now to home,
And joints get rusty, and one's limbs may grow
  More fit to rest than roam.

"But I can stand as yet fair stress and strain;
There's not a little steel beneath the rust;

3

My years mount somewhat, but here's to't again!
   And if I fall, I must.

"God knows that for myself I've scanty care;
Past scrimmages have proved as much to all;
In Eastern lands and South I've had my share
   Both of the blade and ball.

"And where those villains ripped me in the flitch
With their old iron in my early time,
I'm apt at change of wind to feel a twitch,
   Or at a change of clime.

"And what my mirror shows me in the morning
Has more of blotch and wrinkle than of bloom;
My eyes, too, heretofore all glasses scorning,
   Have just a touch of rheum . . .
"Now sounds 'The Girl I've left behind me,'—Ah,
The years, the ardours, wakened by that tune!
Time was when, with the crowd's farewell 'Hurrah!'
   'Twould lift me to the moon.

"But now it's late to leave behind me one
Who if, poor soul, her man goes underground,
Will not recover as she might have done
   In days when hopes abound.

"She's waving from the wharfside, palely grieving,
As down we draw . . . Her tears make little show,
Yet now she suffers more than at my leaving
   Some twenty years ago.

"I pray those left at home will care for her!
I shall come back; I have before; though when
The Girl you leave behind you is a grandmother,
   Things may not be as then."

4

THE GOING OF THE BATTERY

WIVES' LAMENT

(November 2, 1899)

I

O it was sad enough, weak enough, mad enough—
Light in their loving as soldiers can be—
First to risk choosing them, leave alone losing them
Now, in far battle, beyond the South Sea! . . .

II

—Rain came down drenchingly; but we unblenchingly
Trudged on beside them through mirk and through mire,
They stepping steadily—only too readily!—
Scarce as if stepping brought parting-time nigher.

III

Great guns were gleaming there, living things seeming there,
Cloaked in their tar-cloths, upmouthed to the night;
Wheels wet and yellow from axle to felloe,
Throats blank of sound, but prophetic to sight.

IV

Gas-glimmers drearily, blearily, eerily
Lit our pale faces outstretched for one kiss,
While we stood prest to them, with a last quest to them
Not to court perils that honour could miss.

Sharp were those sighs of ours, blinded these eyes of ours,
When at last moved away under the arch
All we loved.   Aid for them each woman prayed for them,
Treading back slowly the track of their march.

VI

Someone said: "Nevermore will they come: evermore
Are they now lost to us." O it was wrong!
Though may be hard their ways, some Hand will guard their
ways,
Bear them through safely, in brief time or long.

VII

—Yet, voices haunting us, daunting us, taunting us,
Hint in the night-time when life beats are low
Other and graver things . . . Hold we to braver things,
Wait we, in trust, what Time's fulness shall show.

AT THE WAR OFFICE, LONDON

(Affixing the Lists of Killed and Wounded: December, 1899)

I

Last year I called this world of gain-givings
The darkest thinkable, and questioned sadly
If my own land could heave its pulse less gladly,

So charged it seemed with circumstance whence springs
   The tragedy of things.

II

Yet at that censured time no heart was rent
Or feature blanched of parent, wife, or daughter
By hourly blazoned sheets of listed slaughter;
Death waited Nature's wont; Peace smiled unshent
   From Ind to Occident.

A CHRISTMAS GHOST-STORY

South of the Line, inland from far Durban,
A mouldering soldier lies—your countryman.
Awry and doubled up are his gray bones,
And on the breeze his puzzled phantom moans
Nightly to clear Canopus: "I would know
By whom and when the All-Earth-gladdening Law
Of Peace, brought in by that Man Crucified,
Was ruled to be inept, and set aside?
And what of logic or of truth appears
In tacking 'Anno Domini' to the years?
Near twenty-hundred livened thus have hied,
But tarries yet the Cause for which He died."

Christmas-eve, 1899

THE DEAD DRUMMER

I

They throw in Drummer Hodge, to rest
  Uncoffined—just as found:
His landmark is a kopje-crest
  That breaks the veldt around;
And foreign constellations west
  Each night above his mound.

II

Young Hodge the Drummer never knew—
  Fresh from his Wessex home—
The meaning of the broad Karoo,
  The Bush, the dusty loam,
And why uprose to nightly view
  Strange stars amid the gloam.

III

Yet portion of that unknown plain
  Will Hodge for ever be;
His homely Northern breast and brain
  Grow up a Southern tree.
And strange-eyed constellations reign
  His stars eternally.

A WIFE IN LONDON

(December, 1899)

I
THE TRAGEDY

She sits in the tawny vapour
That the City lanes have uprolled,
Behind whose webby fold on fold
Like a waning taper
The street-lamp glimmers cold.

A messenger's knock cracks smartly,
Flashed news is in her hand
Of meaning it dazes to understand
Though shaped so shortly:
He—has fallen—in the far South Land . . .

II
THE IRONY

'Tis the morrow; the fog hangs thicker,
The postman nears and goes:
A letter is brought whose lines disclose
By the firelight flicker
His hand, whom the worm now knows:

Fresh—firm—penned in highest feather—
Page-full of his hoped return,
And of home-planned jaunts by brake and burn
In the summer weather,
And of new love that they would learn.

THE SOULS OF THE SLAIN

I

The thick lids of Night closed upon me
Alone at the Bill
Of the Isle by the Race[1] —
Many-caverned, bald, wrinkled of face —
And with darkness and silence the spirit was on me
To brood and be still.

II

No wind fanned the flats of the ocean,
Or promontory sides,
Or the ooze by the strand,
Or the bent-bearded slope of the land,
Whose base took its rest amid everlong motion
Of criss-crossing tides.

III

Soon from out of the Southward seemed nearing
A whirr, as of wings
Waved by mighty-vanned flies,
Or by night-moths of measureless size,
And in softness and smoothness well-nigh beyond hearing
Of corporal things.

IV

And they bore to the bluff, and alighted —

---

[1] The "Race" is the turbulent sea-area off the Bill of Portland, where contrary tides meet.

A dim-discerned train
Of sprites without mould,
Frameless souls none might touch or might hold—
On the ledge by the turreted lantern, farsighted
By men of the main.

V

And I heard them say "Home!" and I knew them
For souls of the felled
On the earth's nether bord
Under Capricorn, whither they'd warred,
And I neared in my awe, and gave heedfulness to them
With breathings inheld.

VI

Then, it seemed, there approached from the northward
A senior soul-flame
Of the like filmy hue:
And he met them and spake: "Is it you,
O my men?" Said they, "Aye! We bear homeward and hearthward
To list to our fame!"

VII

"I've flown there before you," he said then:
"Your households are well;
But—your kin linger less
On your glory arid war-mightiness
Than on dearer things."—"Dearer?" cried these from the dead then,
"Of what do they tell?"

VIII

"Some mothers muse sadly, and murmur
Your doings as boys—

11

Recall the quaint ways
Of your babyhood's innocent days.
Some pray that, ere dying, your faith had grown firmer,
And higher your joys.

IX

"A father broods: 'Would I had set him
To some humble trade,
And so slacked his high fire,
And his passionate martial desire;
Had told him no stories to woo him and whet him
To this due crusade!'"

X

"And, General, how hold out our sweethearts,
Sworn loyal as doves?"
—"Many mourn; many think
It is not unattractive to prink
Them in sables for heroes.   Some fickle and fleet hearts
Have found them new loves."

XI

"And our wives?" quoth another resignedly,
"Dwell they on our deeds?"
—"Deeds of home; that live yet
Fresh as new—deeds of fondness or fret;
Ancient words that were kindly expressed or unkindly,
These, these have their heeds."

XII

—"Alas! then it seems that our glory
Weighs less in their thought
Than our old homely acts,

And the long-ago commonplace facts
Of our lives—held by us as scarce part of our story,
And rated as nought!"

XIII

Then bitterly some: "Was it wise now
To raise the tomb-door
For such knowledge? Away!"
But the rest: "Fame we prized till to-day;
Yet that hearts keep us green for old kindness we prize now
A thousand times more!"

XIV

Thus speaking, the trooped apparitions
Began to disband
And resolve them in two:
Those whose record was lovely and true
Bore to northward for home: those of bitter traditions
Again left the land,

XV

And, towering to seaward in legions,
They paused at a spot
Overbending the Race—
That engulphing, ghast, sinister place—
Whither headlong they plunged, to the fathomless regions
Of myriads forgot.

XVI

And the spirits of those who were homing
Passed on, rushingly,
Like the Pentecost Wind;
And the whirr of their wayfaring thinned

And surceased on the sky, and but left in the gloaming
Sea-mutterings and me.

December 1899

SONG OF THE SOLDIERS' WIVES

I

At last! In sight of home again,
Of home again;
No more to range and roam again
As at that bygone time?
No more to go away from us
And stay from us?—
Dawn, hold not long the day from us,
But quicken it to prime!

II

Now all the town shall ring to them,
Shall ring to them,
And we who love them cling to them
And clasp them joyfully;
And cry, "O much we'll do for you
Anew for you,
Dear Loves!—aye, draw and hew for you,
Come back from oversea."

14

III

Some told us we should meet no more,
Should meet no more;
Should wait, and wish, but greet no more
Your faces round our fires;
That, in a while, uncharily
And drearily
Men gave their lives—even wearily,
Like those whom living tires.

IV

And now you are nearing home again,
Dears, home again;
No more, may be, to roam again
As at that bygone time,
Which took you far away from us
To stay from us;
Dawn, hold not long the day from us,
But quicken it to prime!

THE SICK GOD

I

In days when men had joy of war,
A God of Battles sped each mortal jar;
The peoples pledged him heart and hand,
From Israel's land to isles afar.

II

His crimson form, with clang and chime,
Flashed on each murk and murderous meeting-time,
   And kings invoked, for rape and raid,
   His fearsome aid in rune and rhyme.

III

On bruise and blood-hole, scar and seam,
On blade and bolt, he flung his fulgid beam:
   His haloes rayed the very gore,
   And corpses wore his glory-gleam.

IV

Often an early King or Queen,
And storied hero onward, knew his sheen;
   'Twas glimpsed by Wolfe, by Ney anon,
   And Nelson on his blue demesne.

V

But new light spread. That god's gold nimb
And blazon have waned dimmer and more dim;
   Even his flushed form begins to fade,
   Till but a shade is left of him.

VI

That modern meditation broke
His spell, that penmen's pleadings dealt a stroke,
   Say some; and some that crimes too dire
   Did much to mire his crimson cloak.

VII

Yea, seeds of crescive sympathy
Were sown by those more excellent than he,
   Long known, though long contemned till then—
   The gods of men in amity.

VIII

Souls have grown seers, and thought out-brings
The mournful many-sidedness of things
   With foes as friends, enfeebling ires
   And fury-fires by gaingivings!

IX

He scarce impassions champions now;
They do and dare, but tensely—pale of brow;
   And would they fain uplift the arm
   Of that faint form they know not how.

X

Yet wars arise, though zest grows cold;
Wherefore, at whiles, as 'twere in ancient mould
   He looms, bepatched with paint and lath;
   But never hath he seemed the old!

XI

Let men rejoice, let men deplore.
The lurid Deity of heretofore
   Succumbs to one of saner nod;
   The Battle-god is god no more.

POEMS OF PILGRIMAGE

GENOA AND THE MEDITERRANEAN

(March, 1887)

O epic-famed, god-haunted Central Sea,
Heave careless of the deep wrong done to thee
When from Torino's track I saw thy face first flash on me.

And multimarbled Genova the Proud,
Gleam all unconscious how, wide-lipped, up-browed,
I first beheld thee clad—not as the Beauty but the Dowd.

Out from a deep-delved way my vision lit
On housebacks pink, green, ochreous—where a slit
Shoreward 'twixt row and row revealed the classic blue
through it.

And thereacross waved fishwives' high-hung smocks,
Chrome kerchiefs, scarlet hose, darned underfrocks;
Since when too oft my dreams of thee, O Queen, that frippery
mocks:

Whereat I grieve, Superba! . . . Afterhours
Within Palazzo Doria's orange bowers
Went far to mend these marrings of thy soul-subliming
powers.

But, Queen, such squalid undress none should see,
Those dream-endangering eyewounds no more be
Where lovers first behold thy form in pilgrimage to thee.

SHELLEY'S SKYLARK

(The neighbourhood of Leghorn: March, 1887)

Somewhere afield here something lies
In Earth's oblivious eyeless trust
That moved a poet to prophecies—
A pinch of unseen, unguarded dust

The dust of the lark that Shelley heard,
And made immortal through times to be;—
Though it only lived like another bird,
And knew not its immortality.

Lived its meek life; then, one day, fell—
A little ball of feather and bone;
And how it perished, when piped farewell,
And where it wastes, are alike unknown.

Maybe it rests in the loam I view,
Maybe it throbs in a myrtle's green,
Maybe it sleeps in the coming hue
Of a grape on the slopes of yon inland scene.

Go find it, faeries, go and find
That tiny pinch of priceless dust,
And bring a casket silver-lined,
And framed of gold that gems encrust;

And we will lay it safe therein,
And consecrate it to endless time;
For it inspired a bard to win
Ecstatic heights in thought and rhyme.

IN THE OLD THEATRE, FIESOLE

(April, 1887)

I traced the Circus whose gray stones incline
Where Rome and dim Etruria interjoin,
Till came a child who showed an ancient coin
That bore the image of a Constantine.

She lightly passed; nor did she once opine
How, better than all books, she had raised for me
In swift perspective Europe's history
Through the vast years of Cæsar's sceptred line.

For in my distant plot of English loam
'Twas but to delve, and straightway there to find
Coins of like impress. As with one half blind
Whom common simples cure, her act flashed home
In that mute moment to my opened mind
The power, the pride, the reach of perished Rome.

ROME: ON THE PALATINE

(April, 1887)

We walked where Victor Jove was shrined awhile,
And passed to Livia's rich red mural show,
Whence, thridding cave and Criptoportico,
We gained Caligula's dissolving pile.

And each ranked ruin tended to beguile
The outer sense, and shape itself as though

It wore its marble hues, its pristine glow
Of scenic frieze and pompous peristyle.
When lo, swift hands, on strings nigh over-head,
Began to melodize a waltz by Strauss:
It stirred me as I stood, in Cæsar's house,
Raised the old routs Imperial lyres had led,

And blended pulsing life with lives long done,
Till Time seemed fiction, Past and Present one.

ROME

BUILDING A NEW STREET IN THE ANCIENT QUARTER

(April, 1887)

These numbered cliffs and gnarls of masonry
Outskeleton Time's central city, Rome;
Whereof each arch, entablature, and dome
Lies bare in all its gaunt anatomy.

And cracking frieze and rotten metope
Express, as though they were an open tome
Top-lined with caustic monitory gnome;
"Dunces, Learn here to spell Humanity!"

And yet within these ruins' very shade
The singing workmen shape and set and join
Their frail new mansion's stuccoed cove and quoin
With no apparent sense that years abrade,
Though each rent wall their feeble works invade
Once shamed all such in power of pier and groin.

21

ROME

THE VATICAN—SALA DELLE MUSE

(1887)

I sat in the Muses' Hall at the mid of the day,
And it seemed to grow still, and the people to pass away,
And the chiselled shapes to combine in a haze of sun,
Till beside a Carrara column there gleamed forth One.

She was nor this nor that of those beings divine,
But each and the whole—an essence of all the Nine;
With tentative foot she neared to my halting-place,
A pensive smile on her sweet, small, marvellous face.

"Regarded so long, we render thee sad?" said she.
"Not you," sighed I, "but my own inconstancy!
I worship each and each; in the morning one,
And then, alas! another at sink of sun.

"To-day my soul clasps Form; but where is my troth
Of yesternight with Tune: can one cleave to both?"
—"Be not perturbed," said she. "Though apart in fame,
As I and my sisters are one, those, too, are the same.

—"But my loves go further—to Story, and Dance, and Hymn,
The lover of all in a sun-sweep is fool to whim—
Is swayed like a river-weed as the ripples run!"
—"Nay, wight, thou sway'st not. These are but phases of
one;

"And that one is I; and I am projected from thee,
One that out of thy brain and heart thou causest to be—
Extern to thee nothing. Grieve not, nor thyself becall,
Woo where thou wilt; and rejoice thou canst love at all!"

ROME

AT THE PYRAMID OF CESTIUS
NEAR THE GRAVES OF SHELLEY AND KEATS

(1887)

Who, then, was Cestius,
And what is he to me?—
Amid thick thoughts and memories multitudinous
One thought alone brings he.

I can recall no word
Of anything he did;
For me he is a man who died and was interred
To leave a pyramid

Whose purpose was exprest
Not with its first design,
Nor till, far down in Time, beside it found their rest
Two countrymen of mine.

Cestius in life, maybe,
Slew, breathed out threatening;
I know not. This I know: in death all silently
He does a kindlier thing,

In beckoning pilgrim feet
With marble finger high
To where, by shadowy wall and history-haunted street,
Those matchless singers lie . . .

—Say, then, he lived and died
That stones which bear his name
Should mark, through Time, where two immortal Shades abide;
It is an ample fame.

LAUSANNE

IN GIBBON'S OLD GARDEN: 11–12 P.M.

June 27, 1897

*(The 110th anniversary of the completion of the "Decline and Fall" at the
same hour and place)*

A spirit seems to pass,
Formal in pose, but grave and grand withal:
He contemplates a volume stout and tall,
And far lamps fleck him through the thin acacias.

Anon the book is closed,
With "It is finished!" And at the alley's end
He turns, and soon on me his glances bend;
And, as from earth, comes speech—small, muted, yet composed.

"How fares the Truth now?—Ill?
—Do pens but slily further her advance?
May one not speed her but in phrase askance?
Do scribes aver the Comic to be Reverend still?

"Still rule those minds on earth
At whom sage Milton's wormwood words were hurled:
'Truth like a bastard comes into the world
Never without ill-fame to him who gives her birth'?"

24

ZERMATT

TO THE MATTERHORN

(June–July, 1897)

Thirty-two years since, up against the sun,
Seven shapes, thin atomies to lower sight,
Labouringly leapt and gained thy gabled height,
And four lives paid for what the seven had won.

They were the first by whom the deed was done,
And when I look at thee, my mind takes flight
To that day's tragic feat of manly might,
As though, till then, of history thou hadst none.

Yet ages ere men topped thee, late and soon
Thou watch'dst each night the planets lift and lower;
Thou gleam'dst to Joshua's pausing sun and moon,
And brav'dst the tokening sky when Cæsar's power
Approached its bloody end: yea, saw'st that Noon
When darkness filled the earth till the ninth hour.

THE BRIDGE OF LODI[2]

(Spring, 1887)

I

When of tender mind and body
I was moved by minstrelsy,
And that strain "The Bridge of Lodi"
Brought a strange delight to me.

II

In the battle-breathing jingle
Of its forward-footing tune
I could see the armies mingle,
And the columns cleft and hewn

III

On that far-famed spot by Lodi
Where Napoleon clove his way
To his fame, when like a god he
Bent the nations to his sway.

IV

Hence the tune came capering to me
While I traced the Rhone and Po;
Nor could Milan's Marvel woo me
From the spot englamoured so.

V

And to-day, sunlit and smiling,

---

[2] Pronounce "Loddy."

Here I stand upon the scene,
With its saffron walls, dun tiling,
And its meads of maiden green,

VI

Even as when the trackway thundered
With the charge of grenadiers,
And the blood of forty hundred
Splashed its parapets and piers . . .

VII

Any ancient crone I'd toady
Like a lass in young-eyed prime,
Could she tell some tale of Lodi
At that moving mighty time.

VIII

So, I ask the wives of Lodi
For traditions of that day;
But alas! not anybody
Seems to know of such a fray.

IX

And they heed but transitory
Marketings in cheese and meat,
Till I judge that Lodi's story
Is extinct in Lodi's street.

X

Yet while here and there they thrid them
In their zest to sell and buy,

Let me sit me down amid them
And behold those thousands die . . .

XI

—Not a creature cares in Lodi
How Napoleon swept each arch,
Or where up and downward trod he,
Or for his memorial March!

XII

So that wherefore should I be here,
Watching Adda lip the lea,
When the whole romance to see here
Is the dream I bring with me?

XIII

And why sing "The Bridge of Lodi"
As I sit thereon and swing,
When none shows by smile or nod he
Guesses why or what I sing? . . .

XIV

Since all Lodi, low and head ones,
Seem to pass that story by,
It may be the Lodi-bred ones
Rate it truly, and not I.

XV

Once engrossing Bridge of Lodi,
Is thy claim to glory gone?
Must I pipe a palinody,Or be silent thereupon?

XVI

And if here, from strand to steeple,
Be no stone to fame the fight,
Must I say the Lodi people
Are but viewing crime aright?

XVII

Nay; I'll sing "The Bridge of Lodi" —
That long-loved, romantic thing,
Though none show by smile or nod he
Guesses why and what I sing!

ON AN INVITATION TO THE UNITED STATES

I

My ardours for emprize nigh lost
Since Life has bared its bones to me,
I shrink to seek a modern coast
Whose riper times have yet to be;
Where the new regions claim them free
From that long drip of human tears
Which peoples old in tragedy
Have left upon the centuried years.

II

For, wonning in these ancient lands,

29

Enchased and lettered as a tomb,
And scored with prints of perished hands,
And chronicled with dates of doom,
Though my own Being bear no bloom
I trace the lives such scenes enshrine,
Give past exemplars present room,
And their experience count as mine.

MISCELLANEOUS POEMS

THE MOTHER MOURNS

When mid-autumn's moan shook the night-time,
    And sedges were horny,
And summer's green wonderwork faltered
    On leaze and in lane,

I fared Yell'ham-Firs way, where dimly
    Came wheeling around me
Those phantoms obscure and insistent
    That shadows unchain.

Till airs from the needle-thicks brought me
    A low lamentation,
As 'twere of a tree-god disheartened,
    Perplexed, or in pain.

And, heeding, it awed me to gather
    That Nature herself there
Was breathing in aërie accents,
    With dirgeful refrain,

Weary plaint that Mankind, in these late days,
    Had grieved her by holding
Her ancient high fame of perfection
    In doubt and disdain . . .

— "I had not proposed me a Creature
    (She soughed) so excelling
All else of my kingdom in compass
    And brightness of brain

"As to read my defects with a god-glance,
Uncover each vestige
Of old inadvertence, annunciate
Each flaw and each stain!

"My purpose went not to develop
Such insight in Earthland;
Such potent appraisements affront me,
And sadden my reign!

"Why loosened I olden control here
To mechanize skywards,
Undeeming great scope could outshape in
A globe of such grain?

"Man's mountings of mind-sight I checked not,
Till range of his vision
Has topped my intent, and found blemish
Throughout my domain.

"He holds as inept his own soul-shell—
My deftest achievement—
Contemns me for fitful inventions
Ill-timed and inane:

"No more sees my sun as a Sanct-shape,
My moon as the Night-queen,
My stars as august and sublime ones
That influences rain:

"Reckons gross and ignoble my teaching,
Immoral my story,
My love-lights a lure, that my species
May gather and gain.

"'Give me,' he has said, 'but the matter
And means the gods lot her,

My brain could evolve a creation
More seemly, more sane.'

—"If ever a naughtiness seized me
To woo adulation
From creatures more keen than those crude ones
That first formed my train—

"If inly a moment I murmured,
'The simple praise sweetly,
But sweetlier the sage'—and did rashly
Man's vision unrein,

"I rue it! . . . His guileless forerunners,
Whose brains I could blandish,
To measure the deeps of my mysteries
Applied them in vain.

"From them my waste aimings and futile
I subtly could cover;
'Every best thing,' said they, 'to best purpose
Her powers preordain.'—

"No more such! . . . My species are dwindling,
My forests grow barren,
My popinjays fail from their tappings,
My larks from their strain.

"My leopardine beauties are rarer,
My tusky ones vanish,
My children have aped mine own slaughters
To quicken my wane.

"Let me grow, then, but mildews and mandrakes,
And slimy distortions,
Let nevermore things good and lovely
To me appertain;

"For Reason is rank in my temples,
And Vision unruly,
And chivalrous laud of my cunning
Is heard not again!"

"I SAID TO LOVE"

I said to Love,
"It is not now as in old days
When men adored thee and thy ways
All else above;
Named thee the Boy, the Bright, the One
Who spread a heaven beneath the sun,"
I said to Love.

I said to him,
"We now know more of thee than then;
We were but weak in judgment when,
With hearts abrim,
We clamoured thee that thou would'st please
Inflict on us thine agonies,"
I said to him.

I said to Love,
"Thou art not young, thou art not fair,
No faery darts, no cherub air,
Nor swan, nor dove
Are thine; but features pitiless,
And iron daggers of distress,"
I said to Love.

"Depart then, Love! . . .
—Man's race shall end, dost threaten thou?
The age to come the man of now
Know nothing of?—
We fear not such a threat from thee;
We are too old in apathy!
Mankind shall cease.—So let it be,"
I said to Love.

A COMMONPLACE DAY

The day is turning ghost,
And scuttles from the kalendar in fits and furtively,
   To join the anonymous host
Of those that throng oblivion; ceding his place, maybe,
   To one of like degree.

I part the fire-gnawed logs,
Rake forth the embers, spoil the busy flames, and lay the ends
   Upon the shining dogs;
Further and further from the nooks the twilight's stride
extends,
   And beamless black impends.

Nothing of tiniest worth
Have I wrought, pondered, planned; no one thing asking
blame or praise,
   Since the pale corpse-like birth
Of this diurnal unit, bearing blanks in all its rays—
   Dullest of dull-hued Days!

Wanly upon the panes
The rain slides as have slid since morn my colourless
thoughts; and yet
    Here, while Day's presence wanes,
And over him the sepulchre-lid is slowly lowered and set,
    He wakens my regret.

    Regret—though nothing dear
That I wot of, was toward in the wide world at his prime,
    Or bloomed elsewhere than here,
To die with his decease, and leave a memory sweet, sublime,
    Or mark him out in Time . . .

    —Yet, maybe, in some soul,
In some spot undiscerned on sea or land, some impulse rose,
    Or some intent upstole
Of that enkindling ardency from whose maturer glows
    The world's amendment flows;

    But which, benumbed at birth
By momentary chance or wile, has missed its hope to be
    Embodied on the earth;
And undervoicings of this loss to man's futurity
    May wake regret in me.

AT A LUNAR ECLIPSE

    Thy shadow, Earth, from Pole to Central Sea,
    Now steals along upon the Moon's meek shine
    In even monochrome and curving line
    Of imperturbable serenity.

36

How shall I link such sun-cast symmetry
With the torn troubled form I know as thine,
That profile, placid as a brow divine,
With continents of moil and misery?
And can immense Mortality but throw
So small a shade, and Heaven's high human scheme
Be hemmed within the coasts yon arc implies?

Is such the stellar gauge of earthly show,
Nation at war with nation, brains that teem,
Heroes, and women fairer than the skies?

THE LACKING SENSE

Scene. — A sad-coloured landscape, Waddon Vale

I

"O Time, whence comes the Mother's moody look amid her
labours,
    As of one who all unwittingly has wounded where she
loves?
    Why weaves she not her world-webs to according lutes and
tabors,
With nevermore this too remorseful air upon her face,
        As of angel fallen from grace?"

II

—"Her look is but her story: construe not its symbols keenly:
    In her wonderworks yea surely has she wounded where she
loves.

The sense of ills misdealt for blisses blanks the mien most
queenly,
Self-smitings kill self-joys; and everywhere beneath the sun
 Such deeds her hands have done."

III

—"And how explains thy Ancient Mind her crimes upon her
creatures,
 These fallings from her fair beginnings, woundings where
she loves,
 Into her would-be perfect motions, modes, effects, and
features
Admitting cramps, black humours, wan decay, and baleful
blights,
 Distress into delights?"

IV

—"Ah! know'st thou not her secret yet, her vainly veiled
deficience,
 Whence it comes that all unwittingly she wounds the lives
she loves?
 That sightless are those orbs of hers?—which bar to her
omniscience
Brings those fearful unfulfilments, that red ravage through
her zones
 Whereat all creation groans.

V

"She whispers it in each pathetic strenuous slow endeavour,
 When in mothering she unwittingly sets wounds on what
she loves;
 Yet her primal doom pursues her, faultful, fatal is she ever;
Though so deft and nigh to vision is her facile finger-touch
 That the seers marvel much.

38

"Deal, then, her groping skill no scorn, no note of
malediction;
　Not long on thee will press the hand that hurts the lives it
loves;
　And while she dares dead-reckoning on, in darkness of
affliction,
Assist her where thy creaturely dependence can or may,
　For thou art of her clay."

TO LIFE

O life with the sad seared face,
I weary of seeing thee,
And thy draggled cloak, and thy hobbling pace,
And thy too-forced pleasantry!

I know what thou would'st tell
Of Death, Time, Destiny—
I have known it long, and know, too, well
What it all means for me.

But canst thou not array
Thyself in rare disguise,
And feign like truth, for one mad day,
That Earth is Paradise?

I'll tune me to the mood,
And mumm with thee till eve;
And maybe what as interlude
I feign, I shall believe!

DOOM AND SHE

I

There dwells a mighty pair—
Slow, statuesque, intense—
Amid the vague Immense:
None can their chronicle declare,
Nor why they be, nor whence.

II

Mother of all things made,
Matchless in artistry,
Unlit with sight is she.—
And though her ever well-obeyed
Vacant of feeling he.

III

The Matron mildly asks—
A throb in every word—
"Our clay-made creatures, lord,
How fare they in their mortal tasks
Upon Earth's bounded bord?

IV

"The fate of those I bear,
Dear lord, pray turn and view,
And notify me true;
Shapings that eyelessly I dare
Maybe I would undo.

"Sometimes from lairs of life
Methinks I catch a groan,
Or multitudinous moan,
As though I had schemed a world of strife,
Working by touch alone."

VI

"World-weaver!" he replies,
"I scan all thy domain;
But since nor joy nor pain
Doth my clear substance recognize,
I read thy realms in vain.

VII

"World-weaver! what is Grief?
And what are Right, and Wrong,
And Feeling, that belong
To creatures all who owe thee fief?
What worse is Weak than Strong?" . . .

VIII

—Unlightened, curious, meek,
She broods in sad surmise . . .
—Some say they have heard her sighs
On Alpine height or Polar peak
When the night tempests rise.

THE PROBLEM

Shall we conceal the Case, or tell it—
We who believe the evidence?
Here and there the watch-towers knell it
With a sullen significance,
Heard of the few who hearken intently and carry an eagerly
upstrained sense.

Hearts that are happiest hold not by it;
Better we let, then, the old view reign;
Since there is peace in it, why decry it?
Since there is comfort, why disdain?
Note not the pigment the while that the painting determines
humanity's joy and pain!

THE SUBALTERNS

I

"Poor wanderer," said the leaden sky,
"I fain would lighten thee,
But there be laws in force on high
Which say it must not be."

II

—"I would not freeze thee, shorn one," cried
The North, "knew I but how
To warm my breath, to slack my stride;
But I am ruled as thou."

III

—"To-morrow I attack thee, wight,"
    Said Sickness. "Yet I swear
I bear thy little ark no spite,
    But am bid enter there."

IV

—"Come hither, Son," I heard Death say;
    "I did not will a grave
Should end thy pilgrimage to-day,
    But I, too, am a slave!"

V

We smiled upon each other then,
    And life to me wore less
That fell contour it wore ere when
    They owned their passiveness.

THE SLEEP-WORKER

When wilt thou wake, O Mother, wake and see—
As one who, held in trance, has laboured long
By vacant rote and prepossession strong—
The coils that thou hast wrought unwittingly;

Wherein have place, unrealized by thee,
Fair growths, foul cankers, right enmeshed with wrong,
Strange orchestras of victim-shriek and song,
And curious blends of ache and ecstasy?—

Should that morn come, and show thy opened eyes
All that Life's palpitating tissues feel,
How wilt thou bear thyself in thy surprise?—

Wilt thou destroy, in one wild shock of shame,
Thy whole high heaving firmamental frame,
Or patiently adjust, amend, and heal?

THE BULLFINCHES

Brother Bulleys, let us sing
From the dawn till evening!—
For we know not that we go not
When the day's pale pinions fold
Unto those who sang of old.

When I flew to Blackmoor Vale,
Whence the green-gowned faeries hail,
Roosting near them I could hear them
Speak of queenly Nature's ways,
Means, and moods,—well known to fays.

All we creatures, nigh and far
(Said they there), the Mother's are:
Yet she never shows endeavour
To protect from warrings wild
Bird or beast she calls her child.

Busy in her handsome house
Known as Space, she falls a-drowse;
Yet, in seeming, works on dreaming,

44

While beneath her groping hands
Fiends make havoc in her bands.

How her hussif'ry succeeds
She unknows or she unheeds,
All things making for Death's taking!
—So the green-gowned faeries say
Living over Blackmoor way.

Come then, brethren, let us sing,
From the dawn till evening!—
For we know not that we go not
When the day's pale pinions fold
Unto those who sang of old.

GOD-FORGOTTEN

I towered far, and lo! I stood within
The presence of the Lord Most High,
Sent thither by the sons of earth, to win
Some answer to their cry.

—"The Earth, say'st thou? The Human race?
By Me created? Sad its lot?
Nay: I have no remembrance of such place:
Such world I fashioned not." —

—"O Lord, forgive me when I say
Thou spak'st the word, and mad'st it all." —
"The Earth of men—let me bethink me . . . Yea!
I dimly do recall

"Some tiny sphere I built long back
(Mid millions of such shapes of mine)
So named . . . It perished, surely—not a wrack
    Remaining, or a sign?

"It lost my interest from the first,
My aims therefor succeeding ill;
Haply it died of doing as it durst?"—
    "Lord, it existeth still."—

"Dark, then, its life! For not a cry
Of aught it bears do I now hear;
Of its own act the threads were snapt whereby
    Its plaints had reached mine ear.

"It used to ask for gifts of good,
Till came its severance self-entailed,
When sudden silence on that side ensued,
    And has till now prevailed.

"All other orbs have kept in touch;
Their voicings reach me speedily:
Thy people took upon them overmuch
    In sundering them from me!

"And it is strange—though sad enough—
Earth's race should think that one whose call
Frames, daily, shining spheres of flawless stuff
    Must heed their tainted ball! . . .

"But say'st thou 'tis by pangs distraught,
And strife, and silent suffering?—
Deep grieved am I that injury should be wrought
    Even on so poor a thing!

"Thou should'st have learnt that Not to Mend
For Me could mean but Not to Know:
Hence, Messengers! and straightway put an end
To what men undergo." . . .

Homing at dawn, I thought to see
One of the Messengers standing by.
—Oh, childish thought! . . . Yet oft it comes to me
When trouble hovers nigh.

THE BEDRIDDEN PEASANT

TO AN UNKNOWING GOD

Much wonder I—here long low-laid—
That this dead wall should be
Betwixt the Maker and the made,
Between Thyself and me!

For, say one puts a child to nurse,
He eyes it now and then
To know if better 'tis, or worse,
And if it mourn, and when.

But Thou, Lord, giv'st us men our clay
In helpless bondage thus
To Time and Chance, and seem'st straightway
To think no more of us!

That some disaster cleft Thy scheme
And tore us wide apart,

So that no cry can cross, I deem;
For Thou art mild of heart,

And would'st not shape and shut us in
Where voice can not he heard:
'Tis plain Thou meant'st that we should win
Thy succour by a word.
Might but Thy sense flash down the skies
Like man's from clime to clime,
Thou would'st not let me agonize
Through my remaining time;

But, seeing how much Thy creatures bear —
Lame, starved, or maimed, or blind —
Thou'dst heal the ills with quickest care
Of me and all my kind.

Then, since Thou mak'st not these things be,
But these things dost not know,
I'll praise Thee as were shown to me
The mercies Thou would'st show!

BY THE EARTH'S CORPSE

I

"O Lord, why grievest Thou? —
Since Life has ceased to be
Upon this globe, now cold
As lunar land and sea,
And humankind, and fowl, and fur

48

Are gone eternally,
All is the same to Thee as ere
They knew mortality."

II

"O Time," replied the Lord,
"Thou read'st me ill, I ween;
Were all the same, I should not grieve
At that late earthly scene,
Now blestly past—though planned by me
With interest close and keen!—
Nay, nay: things now are not the same
As they have earlier been.

III

"Written indelibly
On my eternal mind
Are all the wrongs endured
By Earth's poor patient kind,
Which my too oft unconscious hand
Let enter undesigned.
No god can cancel deeds foredone,
Or thy old coils unwind!

IV

"As when, in Noë's days,
I whelmed the plains with sea,
So at this last, when flesh
And herb but fossils be,
And, all extinct, their piteous dust
Revolves obliviously,
That I made Earth, and life, and man,
It still repenteth me!"

MUTE OPINION

I

I traversed a dominion
Whose spokesmen spake out strong
Their purpose and opinion
Through pulpit, press, and song.
I scarce had means to note there
A large-eyed few, and dumb,
Who thought not as those thought there
That stirred the heat and hum.

II

When, grown a Shade, beholding
That land in lifetime trode,
To learn if its unfolding
Fulfilled its clamoured code,
I saw, in web unbroken,
Its history outwrought
Not as the loud had spoken,
But as the mute had thought.

TO AN UNBORN PAUPER CHILD

I

Breathe not, hid Heart: cease silently,
And though thy birth-hour beckons thee,

Sleep the long sleep:
The Doomsters heap
Travails and teens around us here,
And Time-wraiths turn our songsingings to fear.

II

Hark, how the peoples surge and sigh,
And laughters fail, and greetings die:
Hopes dwindle; yea,
Faiths waste away,
Affections and enthusiasms numb;
Thou canst not mend these things if thou dost come.

III

Had I the ear of wombèd souls
Ere their terrestrial chart unrolls,
And thou wert free
To cease, or be,
Then would I tell thee all I know,
And put it to thee: Wilt thou take Life so?

IV

Vain vow! No hint of mine may hence
To theeward fly: to thy locked sense
Explain none can
Life's pending plan:
Thou wilt thy ignorant entry make
Though skies spout fire and blood and nations quake.

V

Fain would I, dear, find some shut plot
Of earth's wide wold for thee, where not
One tear, one qualm,

Should break the calm.
But I am weak as thou and bare;
No man can change the common lot to rare.

VI

Must come and bide. And such are we—
Unreasoning, sanguine, visionary—
That I can hope
Health, love, friends, scope
In full for thee; can dream thou'lt find
Joys seldom yet attained by humankind!

TO FLOWERS FROM ITALY IN WINTER

Sunned in the South, and here to-day;
—If all organic things
Be sentient, Flowers, as some men say,
What are your ponderings?

How can you stay, nor vanish quite
From this bleak spot of thorn,
And birch, and fir, and frozen white
Expanse of the forlorn?

Frail luckless exiles hither brought!
Your dust will not regain
Old sunny haunts of Classic thought
When you shall waste and wane;

But mix with alien earth, be lit
With frigid Boreal flame,

And not a sign remain in it
To tell men whence you came.

ON A FINE MORNING

I

Whence comes Solace?—Not from seeing
What is doing, suffering, being,
Not from noting Life's conditions,
Nor from heeding Time's monitions;
But in cleaving to the Dream,
And in gazing at the gleam
Whereby gray things golden seem.

II

Thus do I this heyday, holding
Shadows but as lights unfolding,
As no specious show this moment
With its irisèd embowment;
But as nothing other than
Part of a benignant plan;
Proof that earth was made for man.

February 1899

TO LIZBIE BROWNE

I

Dear Lizbie Browne,
Where are you now?
In sun, in rain?—
Or is your brow
Past joy, past pain,
Dear Lizbie Browne?

II

Sweet Lizbie Browne
How you could smile,
How you could sing!—
How archly wile
In glance-giving,
Sweet Lizbie Browne!

III

And, Lizbie Browne,
Who else had hair
Bay-red as yours,
Or flesh so fair
Bred out of doors,
Sweet Lizbie Browne?

IV

When, Lizbie Browne,
You had just begun
To be endeared
By stealth to one,

You disappeared
My Lizbie Browne!

V

Ay, Lizbie Browne,
So swift your life,
And mine so slow,
You were a wife
Ere I could show
Love, Lizbie Browne.

VI

Still, Lizbie Browne,
You won, they said,
The best of men
When you were wed . . .
Where went you then,
O Lizbie Browne?

VII

Dear Lizbie Browne,
I should have thought,
"Girls ripen fast,"
And coaxed and caught
You ere you passed,
Dear Lizbie Browne!

VIII

But, Lizbie Browne,
I let you slip;
Shaped not a sign;
Touched never your lip

With lip of mine,
Lost Lizbie Browne!

IX

So, Lizbie Browne,
When on a day
Men speak of me
As not, you'll say,
"And who was he?" —
Yes, Lizbie Browne!

SONG OF HOPE

O sweet To-morrow! —
After to-day
There will away
This sense of sorrow.
Then let us borrow
Hope, for a gleaming
Soon will be streaming,
Dimmed by no gray —
No gray!

While the winds wing us
Sighs from The Gone,
Nearer to dawn
Minute-beats bring us;
When there will sing us
Larks of a glory
Waiting our story

Further anon—
Anon!

Doff the black token,
Don the red shoon,
Right and retune
Viol-strings broken;
Null the words spoken
In speeches of rueing,
The night cloud is hueing,
To-morrow shines soon—
Shines soon!

THE WELL-BELOVED

I wayed by star and planet shine
Towards the dear one's home
At Kingsbere, there to make her mine
When the next sun upclomb.

I edged the ancient hill and wood
Beside the Ikling Way,
Nigh where the Pagan temple stood
In the world's earlier day.

And as I quick and quicker walked
On gravel and on green,
I sang to sky, and tree, or talked
Of her I called my queen.

—"O faultless is her dainty form,
And luminous her mind;

She is the God-created norm
Of perfect womankind!"

A shape whereon one star-blink gleamed
Glode softly by my side,
A woman's; and her motion seemed
The motion of my bride.

And yet methought she'd drawn erstwhile
Adown the ancient leaze,
Where once were pile and peristyle
For men's idolatries.

—"O maiden lithe and lone, what may
Thy name and lineage be,
Who so resemblest by this ray
My darling?—Art thou she?"

The Shape: "Thy bride remains within
Her father's grange and grove."
—"Thou speakest rightly," I broke in,
"Thou art not she I love."

—"Nay: though thy bride remains inside
Her father's walls," said she,
"The one most dear is with thee here,
For thou dost love but me."

Then I: "But she, my only choice,
Is now at Kingsbere Grove?"
Again her soft mysterious voice:
"I am thy only Love."

Thus still she vouched, and still I said,
"O sprite, that cannot be!" . . .
It was as if my bosom bled,
So much she troubled me.

The sprite resumed: "Thou hast transferred
To her dull form awhile
My beauty, fame, and deed, and word,
My gestures and my smile.

"O fatuous man, this truth infer,
Brides are not what they seem;
Thou lovest what thou dreamest her;
I am thy very dream!"

—"O then," I answered miserably,
Speaking as scarce I knew,
"My loved one, I must wed with thee
If what thou say'st be true!"

She, proudly, thinning in the gloom:
"Though, since troth-plight began,
I've ever stood as bride to groom,
I wed no mortal man!"

Thereat she vanished by the Cross
That, entering Kingsbere town,
The two long lanes form, near the fosse
Below the faneless Down.

—When I arrived and met my bride,
Her look was pinched and thin,
As if her soul had shrunk and died,
And left a waste within.

HER REPROACH

Con the dead page as 'twere live love: press on!
Cold wisdom's words will ease thy track for thee;
Aye, go; cast off sweet ways, and leave me wan
To biting blasts that are intent on me.

But if thy object Fame's far summits be,
Whose inclines many a skeleton o'erlies
That missed both dream and substance, stop and see
How absence wears these cheeks and dims these eyes!

It surely is far sweeter and more wise
To water love, than toil to leave anon
A name whose glory-gleam will but advise
Invidious minds to quench it with their own,

And over which the kindliest will but stay
A moment, musing, "He, too, had his day!"

Westbourne Park Villas,
1867

THE INCONSISTENT

I say, "She was as good as fair,"
When standing by her mound;
"Such passing sweetness," I declare,
"No longer treads the ground."
I say, "What living Love can catch
Her bloom and bonhomie,

60

And what in newer maidens match
Her olden warmth to me!"

—There stands within yon vestry-nook
Where bonded lovers sign,
Her name upon a faded book
With one that is not mine.
To him she breathed the tender vow
She once had breathed to me,
But yet I say, "O love, even now
Would I had died for thee!"

A BROKEN APPOINTMENT

You did not come,
And marching Time drew on, and wore me numb.—
Yet less for loss of your dear presence there
Than that I thus found lacking in your make
That high compassion which can overbear
Reluctance for pure lovingkindness' sake
Grieved I, when, as the hope-hour stroked its sum,
You did not come.

You love not me,
And love alone can lend you loyalty;
—I know and knew it. But, unto the store
Of human deeds divine in all but name,
Was it not worth a little hour or more
To add yet this: Once, you, a woman, came
To soothe a time-torn man; even though it be
You love not me?

"BETWEEN US NOW"

Between us now and here—
Two thrown together
Who are not wont to wear
Life's flushest feather—
Who see the scenes slide past,
The daytimes dimming fast,
Let there be truth at last,
Even if despair.

So thoroughly and long
Have you now known me,
So real in faith and strong
Have I now shown me,
That nothing needs disguise
Further in any wise,
Or asks or justifies
A guarded tongue.

Face unto face, then, say,
Eyes mine own meeting,
Is your heart far away,
Or with mine beating?
When false things are brought low,
And swift things have grown slow,
Feigning like froth shall go,
Faith be for aye.

"HOW GREAT MY GRIEF"

(TRIOLET)

How great my grief, my joys how few,
Since first it was my fate to know thee!
—Have the slow years not brought to view
How great my grief, my joys how few,
Nor memory shaped old times anew,
  Nor loving-kindness helped to show thee
How great my grief, my joys how few,
  Since first it was my fate to know thee?

"I NEED NOT GO"

I need not go
Through sleet and snow
To where I know
She waits for me;
She will wait me there
Till I find it fair,
And have time to spare
From company.

When I've overgot
The world somewhat,
When things cost not
Such stress and strain,
Is soon enough
By cypress sough

To tell my Love
I am come again.

And if some day,
When none cries nay,
I still delay
To seek her side,
(Though ample measure
Of fitting leisure
Await my pleasure)
She will riot chide.

What—not upbraid me
That I delayed me,
Nor ask what stayed me
So long? Ah, no!—
New cares may claim me,
New loves inflame me,
She will not blame me,
But suffer it so.

THE COQUETTE, AND AFTER

(TRIOLETS)

I

For long the cruel wish I knew
That your free heart should ache for me
While mine should bear no ache for you;
For, long—the cruel wish!—I knew

How men can feel, and craved to view
My triumph—fated not to be
For long! . . . The cruel wish I knew
That your free heart should ache for me!

II

At last one pays the penalty—
The woman—women always do.
My farce, I found, was tragedy
At last!—One pays the penalty
With interest when one, fancy-free,
Learns love, learns shame . . . Of sinners two
At last one pays the penalty—
The woman—women always do!

A SPOT

In years defaced and lost,
Two sat here, transport-tossed,
Lit by a living love
The wilted world knew nothing of:
Scared momently
By gaingivings,
Then hoping things
That could not be.

Of love and us no trace
Abides upon the place;
The sun and shadows wheel,
Season and season sereward steal;

Foul days and fair
Here, too, prevail,
And gust and gale
As everywhere.

But lonely shepherd souls
Who bask amid these knolls
May catch a faery sound
On sleepy noontides from the ground:
"O not again
Till Earth outwears
Shall love like theirs
Suffuse this glen!"

LONG PLIGHTED

Is it worth while, dear, now,
To call for bells, and sally forth arrayed
For marriage-rites—discussed, decried, delayed
So many years?

Is it worth while, dear, now,
To stir desire for old fond purposings,
By feints that Time still serves for dallyings,
Though quittance nears?

Is it worth while, dear, when
The day being so far spent, so low the sun,
The undone thing will soon be as the done,
And smiles as tears?

Is it worth while, dear, when
Our cheeks are worn, our early brown is gray;
When, meet or part we, none says yea or nay,
Or heeds, or cares?

Is it worth while, dear, since
We still can climb old Yell'ham's wooded mounds
Together, as each season steals its rounds
And disappears?

Is it worth while, dear, since
As mates in Mellstock churchyard we can lie,
Till the last crash of all things low and high
Shall end the spheres?

THE WIDOW

By Mellstock Lodge and Avenue
Towards her door I went,
And sunset on her window-panes
Reflected our intent.

The creeper on the gable nigh
Was fired to more than red
And when I came to halt thereby
"Bright as my joy!" I said.

Of late days it had been her aim
To meet me in the hall;
Now at my footsteps no one came;
And no one to my call.

Again I knocked; and tardily
    An inner step was heard,
And I was shown her presence then
    With scarce an answering word.

She met me, and but barely took
    My proffered warm embrace;
Preoccupation weighed her look,
    And hardened her sweet face.

"To-morrow—could you—would you call?
    Make brief your present stay?
My child is ill—my one, my all!—
    And can't be left to-day."

And then she turns, and gives commands
    As I were out of sound,
Or were no more to her and hers
    Than any neighbour round . . .

—As maid I wooed her; but one came
    And coaxed her heart away,
And when in time he wedded her
    I deemed her gone for aye.

He won, I lost her; and my loss
    I bore I know not how;
But I do think I suffered then
    Less wretchedness than now.

For Time, in taking him, had oped
    An unexpected door
Of bliss for me, which grew to seem
    Far surer than before . . .

Her word is steadfast, and I know
    That plighted firm are we:

But she has caught new love-calls since
She smiled as maid on me!

AT A HASTY WEDDING

(TRIOLET)

If hours be years the twain are blest,
For now they solace swift desire
By bonds of every bond the best,
If hours be years. The twain are blest
Do eastern stars slope never west,
Nor pallid ashes follow fire:
If hours be years the twain are blest,
For now they solace swift desire.

THE DREAM-FOLLOWER

A dream of mine flew over the mead
To the halls where my old Love reigns;
And it drew me on to follow its lead:
And I stood at her window-panes;

And I saw but a thing of flesh and bone
Speeding on to its cleft in the clay;
And my dream was scared, and expired on a moan,
And I whitely hastened away.

HIS IMMORTALITY

I

I saw a dead man's finer part
Shining within each faithful heart
Of those bereft. Then said I: "This must be
    His immortality."

II

I looked there as the seasons wore,
And still his soul continuously upbore
Its life in theirs. But less its shine excelled
    Than when I first beheld.

III

His fellow-yearsmen passed, and then
In later hearts I looked for him again;
And found him—shrunk, alas! into a thin
    And spectral mannikin.

IV

Lastly I ask—now old and chill—
If aught of him remain unperished still;
And find, in me alone, a feeble spark,
    Dying amid the dark.

February 1899

THE TO-BE-FORGOTTEN

I

I heard a small sad sound,
And stood awhile amid the tombs around:
"Wherefore, old friends," said I, "are ye distrest,
Now, screened from life's unrest?"

II

—"O not at being here;
But that our future second death is drear;
When, with the living, memory of us numbs,
And blank oblivion comes!

III

"Those who our grandsires be
Lie here embraced by deeper death than we;
Nor shape nor thought of theirs canst thou descry
With keenest backward eye.

IV

"They bide as quite forgot;
They are as men who have existed not;
Theirs is a loss past loss of fitful breath;
It is the second death.

V

"We here, as yet, each day
Are blest with dear recall; as yet, alway
In some soul hold a loved continuance
Of shape and voice and glance.

"But what has been will be—
First memory, then oblivion's turbid sea;
Like men foregone, shall we merge into those
Whose story no one knows.

VII

"For which of us could hope
To show in life that world-awakening scope
Granted the few whose memory none lets die,
But all men magnify?

VIII

"We were but Fortune's sport;
Things true, things lovely, things of good report
We neither shunned nor sought . . . We see our bourne,
And seeing it we mourn."

WIVES IN THE SERE

I

Never a careworn wife but shows,
If a joy suffuse her,
Something beautiful to those
Patient to peruse her,
Some one charm the world unknows
Precious to a muser,
Haply what, ere years were foes,
Moved her mate to choose her.

II

But, be it a hint of rose
That an instant hues her,
Or some early light or pose
Wherewith thought renews her—
Seen by him at full, ere woes
Practised to abuse her—
Sparely comes it, swiftly goes,
Time again subdues her.

THE SUPERSEDED

I

As newer comers crowd the fore,
  We drop behind.
—We who have laboured long and sore
  Times out of mind,
And keen are yet, must not regret
  To drop behind.

II

Yet there are of us some who grieve
  To go behind;
Staunch, strenuous souls who scarce believe
  Their fires declined,
And know none cares, remembers, spares
  Who go behind.

III

'Tis not that we have unforetold
  The drop behind;
We feel the new must oust the old
  In every kind;
But yet we think, must we, must we,
  Too, drop behind?

AN AUGUST MIDNIGHT

I

A shaded lamp and a waving blind,
And the beat of a clock from a distant floor:
On this scene enter—winged, horned, and spined—
A longlegs, a moth, and a dumbledore;
While 'mid my page there idly stands
A sleepy fly, that rubs its hands . . .

II

Thus meet we five, in this still place,
At this point of time, at this point in space.
—My guests parade my new-penned ink,
Or bang at the lamp-glass, whirl, and sink.
"God's humblest, they!" I muse. Yet why?
They know Earth-secrets that know not I.

Max Gate, 1899

THE CAGED THRUSH FREED AND HOME AGAIN

(VILLANELLE)

"Men know but little more than we,
Who count us least of things terrene,
How happy days are made to be!

"Of such strange tidings what think ye,
O birds in brown that peck and preen?
Men know but little more than we!

"When I was borne from yonder tree
In bonds to them, I hoped to glean
How happy days are made to be,

"And want and wailing turned to glee;
Alas, despite their mighty mien
Men know but little more than we!

"They cannot change the Frost's decree,
They cannot keep the skies serene;
How happy days are made to be

"Eludes great Man's sagacity
No less than ours, O tribes in treen!
Men know but little more than we
How happy days are made to be."

BIRDS AT WINTER NIGHTFALL

(TRIOLET)

Around the house the flakes fly faster,
And all the berries now are gone
From holly and cotoneaster
Around the house. The flakes fly!—faster
Shutting indoors that crumb-outcaster
We used to see upon the lawn
Around the house. The flakes fly faster,
And all the berries now are gone!

Max Gate

THE PUZZLED GAME-BIRDS

(TRIOLET)

They are not those who used to feed us
When we were young—they cannot be—
These shapes that now bereave and bleed us?
They are not those who used to feed us,—
For would they not fair terms concede us?
—If hearts can house such treachery
They are not those who used to feed us
When we were young—they cannot be!

76

WINTER IN DURNOVER FIELD

Scene.—A wide stretch of fallow ground recently sown with wheat, and frozen to iron hardness. Three large birds walking about thereon, and wistfully eyeing the surface. Wind keen from north-east: sky a dull grey.

(TRIOLET)

Rook.—Throughout the field I find no grain;
    The cruel frost encrusts the cornland!
Starling.—Aye: patient pecking now is vain
    Throughout the field, I find . . .
Rook.—No grain!
Pigeon.—Nor will be, comrade, till it rain,
    Or genial thawings loose the lorn land
    Throughout the field.
Rook.—I find no grain:
    The cruel frost encrusts the cornland!

THE LAST CHRYSANTHEMUM

Why should this flower delay so long
    To show its tremulous plumes?
Now is the time of plaintive robin-song,
    When flowers are in their tombs.

Through the slow summer, when the sun
    Called to each frond and whorl

That all he could for flowers was being done,
Why did it not uncurl?

It must have felt that fervid call
Although it took no heed,
Waking but now, when leaves like corpses fall,
And saps all retrocede.

Too late its beauty, lonely thing,
The season's shine is spent,
Nothing remains for it but shivering
In tempests turbulent.

Had it a reason for delay,
Dreaming in witlessness
That for a bloom so delicately gay
Winter would stay its stress?

—I talk as if the thing were born
With sense to work its mind;
Yet it is but one mask of many worn
By the Great Face behind.

THE DARKLING THRUSH

I leant upon a coppice gate
When Frost was spectre-gray,
And Winter's dregs made desolate
The weakening eye of day.
The tangled bine-stems scored the sky
Like strings from broken lyres,

And all mankind that haunted nigh
Had sought their household fires.

The land's sharp features seemed to be
The Century's corpse outleant,
His crypt the cloudy canopy,
The wind his death-lament.
The ancient pulse of germ and birth
Was shrunken hard and dry,
And every spirit upon earth
Seemed fervourless as I.

At once a voice outburst among
The bleak twigs overhead
In a full-hearted evensong
Of joy illimited;
An aged thrush, frail, gaunt, and small,
In blast-beruffled plume,
Had chosen thus to fling his soul
Upon the growing gloom.

So little cause for carollings
Of such ecstatic sound
Was written on terrestrial things
Afar or nigh around,
That I could think there trembled through
His happy good-night air
Some blessed Hope, whereof he knew
And I was unaware.

December 1900

THE COMET AT YALBURY OR YELL'HAM

I

It bends far over Yell'ham Plain,
And we, from Yell'ham Height,
Stand and regard its fiery train,
So soon to swim from sight.

II

It will return long years hence, when
As now its strange swift shine
Will fall on Yell'ham; but not then
On that sweet form of thine.

MAD JUDY

When the hamlet hailed a birth
Judy used to cry:
When she heard our christening mirth
She would kneel and sigh.
She was crazed, we knew, and we
Humoured her infirmity.

When the daughters and the sons
Gathered them to wed,
And we like-intending ones
Danced till dawn was red,
She would rock and mutter, "More
Comers to this stony shore!"

When old Headsman Death laid hands
On a babe or twain,
She would feast, and by her brands
Sing her songs again.
What she liked we let her do,
Judy was insane, we knew.

A WASTED ILLNESS

Through vaults of pain,
Enribbed and wrought with groins of ghastliness,
I passed, and garish spectres moved my brain
To dire distress.

And hammerings,
And quakes, and shoots, and stifling hotness, blent
With webby waxing things and waning things
As on I went.

"Where lies the end
To this foul way?" I asked with weakening breath.
Thereon ahead I saw a door extend—
The door to death.

It loomed more clear:
"At last!" I cried. "The all-delivering door!"
And then, I knew not how, it grew less near
Than theretofore.

And back slid I
Along the galleries by which I came,

And tediously the day returned, and sky,
And life—the same.

And all was well:
Old circumstance resumed its former show,
And on my head the dews of comfort fell
As ere my woe.

I roam anew,
Scarce conscious of my late distress . . . And yet
Those backward steps through pain I cannot view
Without regret.

For that dire train
Of waxing shapes and waning, passed before,
And those grim aisles, must be traversed again
To reach that door.

A MAN

(IN MEMORY OF H. OF M.)

I

In Casterbridge there stood a noble pile,
Wrought with pilaster, bay, and balustrade
In tactful times when shrewd Eliza swayed.—
On burgher, squire, and clown
It smiled the long street down for near a mile

II

But evil days beset that domicile;
The stately beauties of its roof and wall
Passed into sordid hands. Condemned to fall
Were cornice, quoin, and cove,
And all that art had wove in antique style.

III

Among the hired dismantlers entered there
One till the moment of his task untold.
When charged therewith he gazed, and answered bold:
"Be needy I or no,
I will not help lay low a house so fair!

IV

"Hunger is hard. But since the terms be such—
No wage, or labour stained with the disgrace
Of wrecking what our age cannot replace
To save its tasteless soul—
I'll do without your dole. Life is not much!"

V

Dismissed with sneers he backed his tools and went,
And wandered workless; for it seemed unwise
To close with one who dared to criticize
And carp on points of taste:
To work where they were placed rude men were meant.

VI

Years whiled. He aged, sank, sickened, and was not:
And it was said, "A man intractable

And curst is gone." None sighed to hear his knell,
    None sought his churchyard-place;
His name, his rugged face, were soon forgot.

VII

The stones of that fair hall lie far and wide,
    And but a few recall its ancient mould;
    Yet when I pass the spot I long to hold
        As truth what fancy saith:
"His protest lives where deathless things abide!"

THE DAME OF ATHELHALL

I

"Soul! Shall I see thy face," she said,
        "In one brief hour?
And away with thee from a loveless bed
To a far-off sun, to a vine-wrapt bower,
        And be thine own unseparated,
And challenge the world's white glower?"

II

She quickened her feet, and met him where
        They had predesigned:
And they clasped, and mounted, and cleft the air
Upon whirling wheels; till the will to bind
Her life with his made the moments there
        Efface the years behind.

III

Miles slid, and the sight of the port upgrew
  As they sped on;
When slipping its bond the bracelet flew
From her fondled arm. Replaced anon,
 Its cameo of the abjured one drew
  Her musings thereupon.

IV

The gaud with his image once had been
  A gift from him:
And so it was that its carving keen
Refurbished memories wearing dim,
 Which set in her soul a throe of teen,
  And a tear on her lashes' brim.

V

"I may not go!" she at length upspake,
  "Thoughts call me back—
I would still lose all for your dear, dear sake;
My heart is thine, friend! But my track
 I home to Athelhall must take
  To hinder household wrack!"

VI

He appealed. But they parted, weak and wan:
  And he left the shore;
His ship diminished, was low, was gone;
And she heard in the waves as the daytide wore,
 And read in the leer of the sun that shone,
  That they parted for evermore.

VII

She homed as she came, at the dip of eve
On Athel Coomb
Regaining the Hall she had sworn to leave . . .
The house was soundless as a tomb,
And she entered her chamber, there to grieve
Lone, kneeling, in the gloom.

VIII

From the lawn without rose her husband's voice
To one his friend:
"Another her Love, another my choice,
Her going is good. Our conditions mend;
In a change of mates we shall both rejoice;
I hoped that it thus might end!

IX

"A quick divorce; she will make him hers,
And I wed mine.
So Time rights all things in long, long years—
Or rather she, by her bold design!
I admire a woman no balk deters:
She has blessed my life, in fine.

X

"I shall build new rooms for my new true bride,
Let the bygone be:
By now, no doubt, she has crossed the tide
With the man to her mind. Far happier she
In some warm vineland by his side
Than ever she was with me."

THE SEASONS OF HER YEAR

I

Winter is white on turf and tree,
And birds are fled;
But summer songsters pipe to me,
And petals spread,
For what I dreamt of secretly
His lips have said!

II

O 'tis a fine May morn, they say,
And blooms have blown;
But wild and wintry is my day,
My birds make moan;
For he who vowed leaves me to pay
Alone—alone!

THE MILKMAID

Under a daisied bank
There stands a rich red ruminating cow,
And hard against her flank
A cotton-hooded milkmaid bends her brow.

The flowery river-ooze
Upheaves and falls; the milk purrs in the pail;

Few pilgrims but would choose
The peace of such a life in such a vale.

The maid breathes words—to vent,
It seems, her sense of Nature's scenery,
Of whose life, sentiment,
And essence, very part itself is she.

She bends a glance of pain,
And, at a moment, lets escape a tear;
Is it that passing train,
Whose alien whirr offends her country ear?—

Nay! Phyllis does not dwell
On visual and familiar things like these;
What moves her is the spell
Of inner themes and inner poetries:

Could but by Sunday morn
Her gay new gown come, meads might dry to dun,
Trains shriek till ears were torn,
If Fred would not prefer that Other One.

THE LEVELLED CHURCHYARD

"O passenger, pray list and catch
Our sighs and piteous groans,
Half stifled in this jumbled patch
Of wrenched memorial stones!

"We late-lamented, resting here,
Are mixed to human jam,

And each to each exclaims in fear,
'I know not which I am!'

"The wicked people have annexed
The verses on the good;
A roaring drunkard sports the text
Teetotal Tommy should!

"Where we are huddled none can trace,
And if our names remain,
They pave some path or p-ing place
Where we have never lain!

"There's not a modest maiden elf
But dreads the final Trumpet,
Lest half of her should rise herself,
And half some local strumpet!

"From restorations of Thy fane,
From smoothings of Thy sward,
From zealous Churchmen's pick and plane
Deliver us O Lord! Amen!"

1882

THE RUINED MAID

"O 'Melia, my dear, this does everything crown!
Who could have supposed I should meet you in Town?
And whence such fair garments, such prosperi-ty?" —
"O didn't you know I'd been ruined?" said she.

—"You left us in tatters, without shoes or socks,
Tired of digging potatoes, and spudding up docks;
And now you've gay bracelets and bright feathers three!" —
"Yes: that's how we dress when we're ruined," said she.

—"At home in the barton you said 'thee' and 'thou,'
And 'thik oon,' and 'theäs oon,' and 't'other'; but now
Your talking quite fits 'ee for high compa-ny!" —
"Some polish is gained with one's ruin," said she.

—"Your hands were like paws then, your face blue and bleak,
But now I'm bewitched by your delicate cheek,
And your little gloves fit as on any la-dy!" —
"We never do work when we're ruined," said she.

—"You used to call home-life a hag-ridden dream,
And you'd sigh, and you'd sock; but at present you seem
To know not of megrims or melancho-ly!" —
"True. There's an advantage in ruin," said she.

—"I wish I had feathers, a fine sweeping gown,
And a delicate face, and could strut about Town!" —
"My dear—a raw country girl, such as you be,
Isn't equal to that. You ain't ruined," said she.

Westbourne Park Villas, 1866

THE RESPECTABLE BURGHER

ON "THE HIGHER CRITICISM"

Since Reverend Doctors now declare
That clerks and people must prepare
To doubt if Adam ever were;
To hold the flood a local scare;
To argue, though the stolid stare,
That everything had happened ere
The prophets to its happening sware;
That David was no giant-slayer,
Nor one to call a God-obeyer
In certain details we could spare,
But rather was a debonair
Shrewd bandit, skilled as banjo-player:
That Solomon sang the fleshly Fair,
And gave the Church no thought whate'er;
That Esther with her royal wear,
And Mordecai, the son of Jair,
And Joshua's triumphs, Job's despair,
And Balaam's ass's bitter blare;
Nebuchadnezzar's furnace-flare,
And Daniel and the den affair,
And other stories rich and rare,
Were writ to make old doctrine wear
Something of a romantic air:
That the Nain widow's only heir,
And Lazarus with cadaverous glare
(As done in oils by Piombo's care)
Did not return from Sheol's lair:
That Jael set a fiendish snare,
That Pontius Pilate acted square,
That never a sword cut Malchus' ear
And (but for shame I must forbear)

That — — did not reappear! . . .
—Since thus they hint, nor turn a hair,
All churchgoing will I forswear,
And sit on Sundays in my chair,
And read that moderate man Voltaire.

ARCHITECTURAL MASKS

I

There is a house with ivied walls,
And mullioned windows worn and old,
And the long dwellers in those halls
Have souls that know but sordid calls,
And daily dote on gold.

II

In blazing brick and plated show
Not far away a "villa" gleams,
And here a family few may know,
With book and pencil, viol and bow,
Lead inner lives of dreams.

III

The philosophic passers say,
"See that old mansion mossed and fair,
Poetic souls therein are they:
And O that gaudy box! Away,
You vulgar people there."

THE TENANT-FOR-LIFE

The sun said, watching my watering-pot
"Some morn you'll pass away;
These flowers and plants I parch up hot—
Who'll water them that day?

"Those banks and beds whose shape your eye
Has planned in line so true,
New hands will change, unreasoning why
Such shape seemed best to you.

"Within your house will strangers sit,
And wonder how first it came;
They'll talk of their schemes for improving it,
And will not mention your name.

"They'll care not how, or when, or at what
You sighed, laughed, suffered here,
Though you feel more in an hour of the spot
Than they will feel in a year

"As I look on at you here, now,
Shall I look on at these;
But as to our old times, avow
No knowledge—hold my peace! . . .

"O friend, it matters not, I say;
Bethink ye, I have shined
On nobler ones than you, and they
Are dead men out of mind!"

THE KING'S EXPERIMENT

It was a wet wan hour in spring,
And Nature met King Doom beside a lane,
Wherein Hodge trudged, all blithely ballading
The Mother's smiling reign.

"Why warbles he that skies are fair
And coombs alight," she cried, "and fallows gay,
When I have placed no sunshine in the air
Or glow on earth to-day?"

"'Tis in the comedy of things
That such should be," returned the one of Doom;
"Charge now the scene with brightest blazonings,
And he shall call them gloom."

She gave the word: the sun outbroke,
All Froomside shone, the hedgebirds raised a song;
And later Hodge, upon the midday stroke,
Returned the lane along,

Low murmuring: "O this bitter scene,
And thrice accurst horizon hung with gloom!
How deadly like this sky, these fields, these treen,
To trappings of the tomb!"

The Beldame then: "The fool and blind!
Such mad perverseness who may apprehend?" —
"Nay; there's no madness in it; thou shalt find
Thy law there," said her friend.

"When Hodge went forth 'twas to his Love,
To make her, ere this eve, his wedded prize,
And Earth, despite the heaviness above,
Was bright as Paradise.

94

"But I sent on my messenger,
With cunning arrows poisonous and keen,
To take forthwith her laughing life from her,
And dull her little een,

"And white her cheek, and still her breath,
Ere her too buoyant Hodge had reached her side;
So, when he came, he clasped her but in death,
And never as his bride.

"And there's the humour, as I said;
Thy dreary dawn he saw as gleaming gold,
And in thy glistening green and radiant red
Funereal gloom and cold."

THE TREE

AN OLD MAN'S STORY

I

Its roots are bristling in the air
Like some mad Earth-god's spiny hair;
The loud south-wester's swell and yell
Smote it at midnight, and it fell.
Thus ends the tree
Where Some One sat with me.

II

Its boughs, which none but darers trod,

A child may step on from the sod,
And twigs that earliest met the dawn
Are lit the last upon the lawn.
Cart off the tree
Beneath whose trunk sat we!

III

Yes, there we sat: she cooed content,
And bats ringed round, and daylight went;
The gnarl, our seat, is wrenched and sunk,
Prone that queer pocket in the trunk
Where lay the key
To her pale mystery.

IV

"Years back, within this pocket-hole
I found, my Love, a hurried scrawl
Meant not for me," at length said I;
"I glanced thereat, and let it lie:
The words were three—
'Beloved, I agree.'

V

"Who placed it here; to what request
It gave assent, I never guessed.
Some prayer of some hot heart, no doubt,
To some coy maiden hereabout,
Just as, maybe,
With you, Sweet Heart, and me."

VI

She waited, till with quickened breath

She spoke, as one who banisheth
Reserves that lovecraft heeds so well,
To ease some mighty wish to tell:
"'Twas I," said she,
"Who wrote thus clinchingly.

VII

"My lover's wife—aye, wife!—knew nought
Of what we felt, and bore, and thought . . .
He'd said: 'I wed with thee or die:
She stands between, 'tis true. But why?
Do thou agree,
And—she shalt cease to be.'

VIII

"How I held back, how love supreme
Involved me madly in his scheme
Why should I say? . . . I wrote assent
(You found it hid) to his intent . . .
She—died . . . But he
Came not to wed with me.

IX

"O shrink not, Love!—Had these eyes seen
But once thine own, such had not been!
But we were strangers . . . Thus the plot
Cleared passion's path.—Why came he not
To wed with me? . . .
He wived the gibbet-tree."

X

—Under that oak of heretofore

Sat Sweetheart mine with me no more:
By many a Fiord, and Strom, and Fleuve
Have I since wandered . . . Soon, for love,
Distraught went she—
'Twas said for love of me.

HER LATE HUSBAND

(KING'S-HINTOCK, 182–.)

"No—not where I shall make my own;
But dig his grave just by
The woman's with the initialed stone—
As near as he can lie—
After whose death he seemed to ail,
Though none considered why.

"And when I also claim a nook,
And your feet tread me in,
Bestow me, under my old name,
Among my kith and kin,
That strangers gazing may not dream
I did a husband win."

"Widow, your wish shall be obeyed;
Though, thought I, certainly
You'd lay him where your folk are laid,
And your grave, too, will be,
As custom hath it; you to right,
And on the left hand he."

"Aye, sexton; such the Hintock rule,
And none has said it nay;
But now it haps a native here
Eschews that ancient way . . .
And it may be, some Christmas night,
When angels walk, they'll say:

"'O strange interment! Civilized lands
Afford few types thereof;
Here is a man who takes his rest
Beside his very Love,
Beside the one who was his wife
In our sight up above!'"

THE SELF-UNSEEING

Here is the ancient floor,
Footworn and hollowed and thin,
Here was the former door
Where the dead feet walked in.

She sat here in her chair,
Smiling into the fire;
He who played stood there,
Bowing it higher and higher.

Childlike, I danced in a dream;
Blessings emblazoned that day
Everything glowed with a gleam;
Yet we were looking away!

DE PROFUNDIS

I

"Percussus sum sicut foenum, et aruit cor meum."

—Ps. ci

Wintertime nighs;
But my bereavement-pain
It cannot bring again:
Twice no one dies.

Flower-petals flee;
But, since it once hath been,
No more that severing scene
Can harrow me.

Birds faint in dread:
I shall not lose old strength
In the lone frost's black length:
Strength long since fled!

Leaves freeze to dun;
But friends can not turn cold
This season as of old
For him with none.

Tempests may scath;
But love can not make smart
Again this year his heart
Who no heart hath.

Black is night's cope;
But death will not appal

One who, past doubtings all,
Waits in unhope.

II

"Considerabam ad dexteram, et videbam; et non erat qui
cognosceret me . . . Non est qui requirat animam meam." —Ps. cxli.

When the clouds' swoln bosoms echo back the shouts of the
many and strong
That things are all as they best may be, save a few to be right
ere long,
And my eyes have not the vision in them to discern what to
these is so clear,
The blot seems straightway in me alone; one better he were
not here.

The stout upstanders say, All's well with us: ruers have
nought to rue!
And what the potent say so oft, can it fail to be somewhat
true?
Breezily go they, breezily come; their dust smokes around
their career,
Till I think I am one born out of due time, who has no calling
here.

Their dawns bring lusty joys, it seems; their eves exultance
sweet;
Our times are blessed times, they cry: Life shapes it as is most
meet,
And nothing is much the matter; there are many smiles to a
tear;
Then what is the matter is I, I say. Why should such an one
be here? . . .

Let him to whose ears the low-voiced Best seems stilled by
the clash of the First,

Who holds that if way to the Better there be, it exacts a full look at the Worst,

Who feels that delight is a delicate growth cramped by crookedness, custom, and fear,

Get him up and be gone as one shaped awry; he disturbs the order here.

1895–96

III

"Heu mihi, quia incolatus meus prolongatus est! Habitavi cum habitantibus Cedar; multum incola fuit aninia mea."—Ps. cxix.

There have been times when I well might have passed and the ending have come—

Points in my path when the dark might have stolen on me, artless, unrueing—

Ere I had learnt that the world was a welter of futile doing:

Such had been times when I well might have passed, and the ending have come!

Say, on the noon when the half-sunny hours told that April was nigh,

And I upgathered and cast forth the snow from the crocus-border,

Fashioned and furbished the soil into a summer-seeming order,

Glowing in gladsome faith that I quickened the year thereby.

Or on that loneliest of eves when afar and benighted we stood,

She who upheld me and I, in the midmost of Egdon together,

Confident I in her watching and ward through the blackening heather,

Deeming her matchless in might and with measureless scope endued.

102

Or on that winter-wild night when, reclined by the chimney-nook quoin,

Slowly a drowse overgat me, the smallest and feeblest of folk there,

Weak from my baptism of pain; when at times and anon I awoke there—

Heard of a world wheeling on, with no listing or longing to join.

Even then! while unweeting that vision could vex or that knowledge could numb,

That sweets to the mouth in the belly are bitter, and tart, and untoward,

Then, on some dim-coloured scene should my briefly raised curtain have lowered,

Then might the Voice that is law have said "Cease!" and the ending have come.

1896

THE CHURCH-BUILDER

I

The church flings forth a battled shade
Over the moon-blanched sward;
The church; my gift; whereto I paid
My all in hand and hoard:
Lavished my gains
With stintless pains
To glorify the Lord.

II

I squared the broad foundations in
Of ashlared masonry;
I moulded mullions thick and thin,
Hewed fillet and ogee;
I circleted
Each sculptured head
With nimb and canopy.

III

I called in many a craftsmaster
To fix emblazoned glass,
To figure Cross and Sepulchre
On dossal, boss, and brass.
My gold all spent,
My jewels went
To gem the cups of Mass.

IV

I borrowed deep to carve the screen
And raise the ivoried Rood;
I parted with my small demesne
To make my owings good.
Heir-looms unpriced
I sacrificed,
Until debt-free I stood.

V

So closed the task. "Deathless the Creed
Here substanced!" said my soul:
"I heard me bidden to this deed,
And straight obeyed the call.

Illume this fane,
That not in vain
I build it, Lord of all!"

VI

But, as it chanced me, then and there
Did dire misfortunes burst;
My home went waste for lack of care,
My sons rebelled and curst;
Till I confessed
That aims the best
Were looking like the worst.

VII

Enkindled by my votive work
No burning faith I find;
The deeper thinkers sneer and smirk,
And give my toil no mind;
From nod and wink
I read they think
That I am fool and blind.

VIII

My gift to God seems futile, quite;
The world moves as erstwhile;
And powerful wrong on feeble right
Tramples in olden style.
My faith burns down,
I see no crown;
But Cares, and Griefs, and Guile.

IX

So now, the remedy? Yea, this:
I gently swing the door
Here, of my fane—no soul to wis—
And cross the patterned floor
To the rood-screen
That stands between
The nave and inner chore.

X

The rich red windows dim the moon,
But little light need I;
I mount the prie-dieu, lately hewn
From woods of rarest dye;
Then from below
My garment, so,
I draw this cord, and tie

XI

One end thereof around the beam
Midway 'twixt Cross and truss:
I noose the nethermost extreme,
And in ten seconds thus
I journey hence—
To that land whence
No rumour reaches us.

XII

Well: Here at morn they'll light on one
Dangling in mockery
Of what he spent his substance on
Blindly and uselessly! . . .

"He might," they'll say,
"Have built, some way.
A cheaper gallows-tree!"

THE LOST PYX

A MEDIÆVAL LEGEND[3]

Some say the spot is banned; that the pillar Cross-and-Hand
Attests to a deed of hell;
But of else than of bale is the mystic tale
That ancient Vale-folk tell.

Ere Cernel's Abbey ceased hereabout there dwelt a priest,
(In later life sub-prior
Of the brotherhood there, whose bones are now bare
In the field that was Cernel choir).

One night in his cell at the foot of yon dell
The priest heard a frequent cry:
"Go, father, in haste to the cot on the waste,
And shrive a man waiting to die."

Said the priest in a shout to the caller without,
"The night howls, the tree-trunks bow;

---

[3] On a lonely table-land above the Vale of Blackmore, between High-Stoy and Bubb-Down hills, and commanding in clear weather views that extend from the English to the Bristol Channel, stands a pillar, apparently mediæval, called Cross-and-Hand or Christ-in-Hand. Among other stories of its origin a local tradition preserves the one here given.

One may barely by day track so rugged a way,
    And can I then do so now?"

No further word from the dark was heard,
    And the priest moved never a limb;
And he slept and dreamed; till a Visage seemed
    To frown from Heaven at him.

In a sweat he arose; and the storm shrieked shrill,
    And smote as in savage joy;
While High-Stoy trees twanged to Bubb-Down Hill,
    And Bubb-Down to High-Stoy.

There seemed not a holy thing in hail,
    Nor shape of light or love,
From the Abbey north of Blackmore Vale
    To the Abbey south thereof.

Yet he plodded thence through the dark immense,
    And with many a stumbling stride
Through copse and briar climbed nigh and nigher
    To the cot and the sick man's side.

When he would have unslung the Vessels uphung
    To his arm in the steep ascent,
He made loud moan: the Pyx was gone
    Of the Blessed Sacrament.

Then in dolorous dread he beat his head:
    "No earthly prize or pelf
Is the thing I've lost in tempest tossed,
    But the Body of Christ Himself!"

He thought of the Visage his dream revealed,
    And turned towards whence he came,
Hands groping the ground along foot-track and field,
    And head in a heat of shame.

Till here on the hill, betwixt vill and vill,
He noted a clear straight ray
Stretching down from the sky to a spot hard by,
Which shone with the light of day.

And gathered around the illumined ground
Were common beasts and rare,
All kneeling at gaze, and in pause profound
Attent on an object there.

'Twas the Pyx, unharmed 'mid the circling rows
Of Blackmore's hairy throng,
Whereof were oxen, sheep, and does,
And hares from the brakes among;

And badgers grey, and conies keen,
And squirrels of the tree,
And many a member seldom seen
Of Nature's family.

The ireful winds that scoured and swept
Through coppice, clump, and dell,
Within that holy circle slept
Calm as in hermit's cell.

Then the priest bent likewise to the sod
And thanked the Lord of Love,
And Blessed Mary, Mother of God,
And all the saints above.

And turning straight with his priceless freight,
He reached the dying one,
Whose passing sprite had been stayed for the rite
Without which bliss hath none.

And when by grace the priest won place,

And served the Abbey well,
He reared this stone to mark where shone
    That midnight miracle.

TESS'S LAMENT

I

I would that folk forgot me quite,
    Forgot me quite!
I would that I could shrink from sight,
    And no more see the sun.
Would it were time to say farewell,
To claim my nook, to need my knell,
Time for them all to stand and tell
    Of my day's work as done.

II

Ah! dairy where I lived so long,
    I lived so long;
Where I would rise up stanch and strong,
    And lie down hopefully.
'Twas there within the chimney-seat
He watched me to the clock's slow beat—
Loved me, and learnt to call me sweet,
    And whispered words to me.

III

And now he's gone; and now he's gone; . . .

And now he's gone!
The flowers we potted p'rhaps are thrown
To rot upon the farm.
And where we had our supper-fire
May now grow nettle, dock, and briar,
And all the place be mould and mire
So cozy once and warm.

IV

And it was I who did it all,
Who did it all;
'Twas I who made the blow to fall
On him who thought no guile.
Well, it is finished—past, and he
Has left me to my misery,
And I must take my Cross on me
For wronging him awhile.

V

How gay we looked that day we wed,
That day we wed!
"May joy be with ye!" all o'm said
A standing by the durn.
I wonder what they say o's now,
And if they know my lot; and how
She feels who milks my favourite cow,
And takes my place at churn!

VI

It wears me out to think of it,
To think of it;
I cannot bear my fate as writ,
I'd have my life unbe;

Would turn my memory to a blot,
　Make every relic of me rot,
My doings be as they were not,
　And what they've brought to me!

THE SUPPLANTER

A TALE

I

He bends his travel-tarnished feet
　To where she wastes in clay:
From day-dawn until eve he fares
　Along the wintry way;
From day-dawn until eve repairs
　Unto her mound to pray.

II

"Are these the gravestone shapes that meet
　My forward-straining view?
Or forms that cross a window-blind
　In circle, knot, and queue:
Gay forms, that cross and whirl and wind
　To music throbbing through?" —

III

"The Keeper of the Field of Tombs
　Dwells by its gateway-pier;
He celebrates with feast and dance

His daughter's twentieth year:
He celebrates with wine of France
The birthday of his dear." —

IV

"The gates are shut when evening glooms:
Lay down your wreath, sad wight;
To-morrow is a time more fit
For placing flowers aright:
The morning is the time for it;
Come, wake with us to-night!" —

V

He grounds his wreath, and enters in,
And sits, and shares their cheer. —
"I fain would foot with you, young man,
Before all others here;
I fain would foot it for a span
With such a cavalier!"

VI

She coaxes, clasps, nor fails to win
His first-unwilling hand:
The merry music strikes its staves,
The dancers quickly band;
And with the damsel of the graves
He duly takes his stand.

VII

"You dance divinely, stranger swain,
Such grace I've never known.
O longer stay! Breathe not adieu
And leave me here alone!

O longer stay: to her be true
Whose heart is all your own!" —

VIII

"I mark a phantom through the pane,
That beckons in despair,
Its mouth all drawn with heavy moan—
Her to whom once I sware!" —
"Nay; 'tis the lately carven stone
Of some strange girl laid there!" —

IX

"I see white flowers upon the floor
Betrodden to a clot;
My wreath were they?" — "Nay; love me much,
Swear you'll forget me not!
'Twas but a wreath! Full many such
Are brought here and forgot."

****

X

The watches of the night grow hoar,
He rises ere the sun;
"Now could I kill thee here!" he says,
"For winning me from one
Who ever in her living days
Was pure as cloistered nun!"

XI

She cowers, and he takes his track
Afar for many a mile,

For evermore to be apart
From her who could beguile
His senses by her burning heart,
And win his love awhile.

XII

A year: and he is travelling back
To her who wastes in clay;
From day-dawn until eve he fares
Along the wintry way,
From day-dawn until eve repairs
Unto her mound to pray.

XIII

And there he sets him to fulfil
His frustrate first intent:
And lay upon her bed, at last,
The offering earlier meant:
When, on his stooping figure, ghast
And haggard eyes are bent.

XIV

"O surely for a little while
You can be kind to me!
For do you love her, do you hate,
She knows not—cares not she:
Only the living feel the weight
Of loveless misery!

XV

"I own my sin; I've paid its cost,
Being outcast, shamed, and bare:

I give you daily my whole heart,
Your babe my tender care,
I pour you prayers; and aye to part
Is more than I can bear!"

XVI

He turns—unpitying, passion-tossed;
"I know you not!" he cries,
"Nor know your child. I knew this maid,
But she's in Paradise!"
And swiftly in the winter shade
He breaks from her and flies.

IMITATIONS, ETC.

SAPPHIC FRAGMENT

"Thou shalt be—Nothing."—Omar Khayyám.

"Tombless, with no remembrance."—W. Shakespeare.

Dead shalt thou lie; and nought
　Be told of thee or thought,
For thou hast plucked not of the Muses' tree:
　And even in Hades' halls
　Amidst thy fellow-thralls
No friendly shade thy shade shall company!

CATULLUS: XXXI

(After passing Sirmione, April 1887)

Sirmio, thou dearest dear of strands
That Neptune strokes in lake and sea,
With what high joy from stranger lands
Doth thy old friend set foot on thee!
Yea, barely seems it true to me
That no Bithynia holds me now,
But calmly and assuringly
Around me stretchest homely Thou.

Is there a scene more sweet than when
Our clinging cares are undercast,
And, worn by alien moils and men,
The long untrodden sill repassed,
We press the pined for couch at last,
And find a full repayment there?
Then hail, sweet Sirmio; thou that wast,
And art, mine own unrivalled Fair!

AFTER SCHILLER

Knight, a true sister-love
This heart retains;
Ask me no other love,
That way lie pains!

Calm must I view thee come,
Calm see thee go;
Tale-telling tears of thine
I must not know!

SONG FROM HEINE

I scanned her picture dreaming,
Till each dear line and hue
Was imaged, to my seeming,
As if it lived anew.

Her lips began to borrow
Their former wondrous smile;
Her fair eyes, faint with sorrow,
Grew sparkling as erstwhile.

Such tears as often ran not
Ran then, my love, for thee;
And O, believe I cannot
That thou are lost to me!

FROM VICTOR HUGO

Child, were I king, I'd yield my royal rule,
My chariot, sceptre, vassal-service due,
My crown, my porphyry-basined waters cool,
My fleets, whereto the sea is but a pool,
For a glance from you!

Love, were I God, the earth and its heaving airs,
Angels, the demons abject under me,
Vast chaos with its teeming womby lairs,
Time, space, all would I give—aye, upper spheres,
For a kiss from thee!

CARDINAL BEMBO'S EPITAPH ON RAPHAEL

Here's one in whom Nature feared—faint at such vying—
Eclipse while he lived, and decease at his dying.

RETROSPECT

"I HAVE LIVED WITH SHADES"

I

I have lived with shades so long,
And talked to them so oft,
Since forth from cot and croft
I went mankind among,
That sometimes they
In their dim style
Will pause awhile
To hear my say;

II

And take me by the hand,
And lead me through their rooms
In the To-be, where Dooms
Half-wove and shapeless stand:
And show from there
The dwindled dust
And rot and rust
Of things that were.

III

"Now turn," spake they to me
One day: "Look whence we came,
And signify his name
Who gazes thence at thee." —
— "Nor name nor race
Know I, or can,"

I said, "Of man
So commonplace.

IV

"He moves me not at all;
I note no ray or jot
Of rareness in his lot,
Or star exceptional.
Into the dim
Dead throngs around
He'll sink, nor sound
Be left of him."

V

"Yet," said they, "his frail speech,
Hath accents pitched like thine—
Thy mould and his define
A likeness each to each—
But go! Deep pain
Alas, would be
His name to thee,
And told in vain!"

Feb. 2, 1899

MEMORY AND I

"O memory, where is now my youth,
Who used to say that life was truth?"

"I saw him in a crumbled cot
   Beneath a tottering tree;
That he as phantom lingers there
   Is only known to me."

"O Memory, where is now my joy,
Who lived with me in sweet employ?"

"I saw him in gaunt gardens lone,
   Where laughter used to be;
That he as phantom wanders there
   Is known to none but me."

"O Memory, where is now my hope,
Who charged with deeds my skill and scope?"

"I saw her in a tomb of tomes,
   Where dreams are wont to be;
That she as spectre haunteth there
   Is only known to me."

"O Memory, where is now my faith,
One time a champion, now a wraith?"

"I saw her in a ravaged aisle,
   Bowed down on bended knee;
That her poor ghost outflickers there
   Is known to none but me."

"O Memory, where is now my love,
That rayed me as a god above?"

"I saw him by an ageing shape
   Where beauty used to be;
That his fond phantom lingers there
   Is only known to me."

ΑΓΝΩΣΤΩ. ΘΕΩ.

Long have I framed weak phantasies of Thee,
O Willer masked and dumb!
Who makest Life become,—
As though by labouring all-unknowingly,
Like one whom reveries numb.

How much of consciousness informs Thy will
Thy biddings, as if blind,
Of death-inducing kind,
Nought shows to us ephemeral ones who fill
But moments in Thy mind.

Perhaps Thy ancient rote-restricted ways
Thy ripening rule transcends;
That listless effort tends
To grow percipient with advance of days,
And with percipience mends.

For, in unwonted purlieus, far and nigh,
At whiles or short or long,
May be discerned a wrong
Dying as of self-slaughter; whereat I
Would raise my voice in song.